MW00892528

Copyright © 2018 by Trish Madson
Illustrations copyright © 2018 by Chorkung Kung
All rights reserved.

Published by Familius™ LLC, www.familius.com

Familius books are available at special discounts for bulk purchases, whether for sales promotions
or for family or corporate use. For more information, contact Familius Sales at 559-876-2170 or
email orders@familius.com.

Reproduction of this book in any manner, in whole or in part,
without written permission of the publisher is prohibited.

Library of Congress Cataloging-in-Publication Data
2018937162   ISBN 9781641700412   eISBN 9781641700924

Printed in China

Book and jacket design by David Miles

10 9 8 7 6 5 4 3 2 1

First Edition

12 Little Elves visit COLORADO

by TRISH MADSON

ILLUSTRATIONS BY
CHORKUNG KUNG

FAMILIUS

'Twas Christmas in Colorado
and 12 elves were sent
to see who was sleeping . . .

away the elves went!

In each home was nestled each girl and each boy,

while Centennial State visions brought everyone joy.

The lovely blue spruce trees
donned holiday lights,

and some bighorn sheep had
a big snowball fight.

Tattered Cover was stocked
full of elf books to spare,
while magic elf dust
swirled all through the air.

Rides at Elitch Gardens
were an absolute ball,

but the Kit Carson carousel
outshined them all.

At the Garden of the Gods
was a beautiful sight,
so the elves took a hike
with their gear packed up tight.

There were glistening snowflakes on
frosty Pikes Peak,
while the elves rode the train
for what felt like a week.

From atop Republic Plaza
you can see the Mile High City
all decorated with lights—
so festive and pretty.

The Denver Zoo animals
danced a holiday jive
while they waited for
Santa's red sleigh to arrive.

In the Fryingpan River,
cutthroat trout wore big bows
as the elves gave them gifts
with jolly "Ho-ho-ho"s.

The Red Rocks Amphitheatre
was the perfect site
to sing Christmas carols like
"O Holy Night."

Goodnight, Colorado.
You're all fast asleep,
but there's just one more house
that the elves want to see . . .

Hurry to bed now
and shut your eyes tight.
Merry Christmas, dear Colorado.
12 elves say good night!